STEP
BROTHER
with Benefits

MIA CLARK

ISBN: 1511635991
ISBN-13: 978-1511635998

Book design by Cerys du Lys
Cover design by Cerys du Lys
Cover Image © Depositphotos | avgustino

Cherrylily.com

DEDICATION

Thank you to Ethan and Cerys for helping me with this book and everything involved in the process. This is a dream come true and I wouldn't have been able to do it without them. Thank you, thank you!

CONTENTS

ACKNOWLEDGMENTS

Thank you for taking a chance on my book!

I know that the stepbrother theme can be a difficult one to deal with for a lot of people for a variety of reasons, and so I took that into consideration when I was writing this. While this is a story about forbidden love, it's also a story about two people becoming friends, too. Sometimes you need someone to push you in your life, even when you think everything is fine. Sometimes you need someone to be there, even when you don't know how to ask them to stay with you.

This is that kind of story. It is about two people becoming friends, and then becoming lovers. The forbidden aspects add tension, but it's more than that, too. Sometimes opposites attract in the best way possible. I hope you enjoy my books!

STEPBROTHER WITH BENEFITS

1 - Ashley

I DON'T KNOW WHAT POSSESSED ME to tell Ethan what I told him, but I feel bolder and stronger with him around. Maybe it's because he doesn't judge me. I don't know if he judges anyone, though. He has a tendency of coming across as very carefree and indifferent, but in an interested way if that makes any sense? It doesn't make sense to me, but that's still what it seems like.

And so... I just tell him, and he looks at me funny for a second, then he laughs.

"Yeah, alright," he says. "Right here, or what?"

"No! Um... no..." I say. This is more difficult than I thought.

"Alright," he says, smiling, shrugging. "Tell me how you want to do this?"

"Can we go upstairs?" I ask. "To our own rooms. We can get towels there, then meet back down here. We need towels anyways, right? To go swimming, I mean."

"Yeah, good idea," Ethan says. "You sure about his? We don't have to."

I nod quick. "No, I want to. I'm just nervous, that's all."

He grins and gives me a quick peck on the cheek. "No need to be nervous, Princess. It's just you and me, right?"

It's true. It's just us. We're safe here. No one can hurt us or judge us or say anything.

That's what I want to think, except Ethan has a habit of hurting people, too. I don't think he does it on purpose. *Now* I don't think he does it on purpose, at least. It just seems to happen. It follows him around like a dog's tail, wagging and knocking over expensive vases. Dogs don't mean to do that, but it doesn't make them any less blameless, now does it?

Ethan takes my hand in his and leads me to the stairs, then up them. At the top, we both look towards our respective rooms. Mine is the opposite way down the hall from his.

"See you soon," Ethan says with a cheeky smile.

I smile back; I can't help myself. "Thank you," I say.

He brushes off my appreciation. It's nothing. I don't need to thank him.

I scurry to my room and close the door behind me, then flop down on my bed. I'm still just wearing my panties and Ethan's shirt, but soon I'll be in my swimwear, um... if you can even call it that?

I have a bunch of different bathing suits in my dresser: bikinis that I only wear when it's me and my mom, or one-pieces the rest of the time. Now that I think about it, I don't think I've ever worn a bathing suit around Ethan. Maybe he's seen me in one from time to time on accident, but never intentionally. He swims all the time, though. I've seen him half-naked quite a bit.

And now I've seen him naked. Also quite a bit.

Well, time to change! I try to hype myself up for it, but I'm still nervous. I don't have to do this, I tell myself. I can chicken out of it. He won't make fun of me for that. He won't get upset at me. He won't. I know he won't, but...

Nope! I'm going to do it anyways! My bathing suit is...

Nothing. That's what I told him. Why don't we go skinny dipping?

I've never gone skinny dipping before. I've always kind of wanted to, but I've never had anyone to go with.

I slip my panties down my legs and let them pool on the ground, then I lift Ethan's shirt up over my head and toss it to the floor by my feet.

There. Done. I'm changed. That was easy. I laugh, giddy with excitement.

Sneaking into my bathroom quick, I grab a towel for later when I need to dry off. It's big and fluffy and suddenly I have a partial change of heart. Am I really going to go swimming naked? Um, yes. Yes, I am. I feel weird walking around the house naked, though. I don't know why, I just do.

I wrap the towel around my body, covering myself like I've just stepped out of the shower. Yes, this is alright. It's fine. I can go like this. I tiptoe out of my room, quiet, and close my door then head downstairs to the pool. Ethan isn't there yet, so I just wait at the edge, poking my foot over and dipping my toes into the water.

It's a heated pool and it's warm out, so the water is nice. I do like swimming, I just get self-conscious sometimes. Maybe I should get in before Ethan comes, so I can hide under the water? Sort of. I know he can still see me naked then, but it's kind of concealing a little bit, right?

I don't have time, though. I hear the slider door to the house open, and when I spin around, there he is.

Ethan is not wearing a towel. He has one draped over his shoulder, but it's definitely not covering anything. Nothing at all. I stare. *Oh my...*

2 - Ethan

ALRIGHT, I thought we were swimming naked? I don't know anymore. Yeah, she's probably naked under that towel, but she's still got a towel on, and I can't see her sexy as fuck body beneath it, which is a real disappointment. Yeah, no sex, I get it. Sorry, I'm still hard for her. I can't help it. I can't stop. I'll be good, though. I'll contain myself.

Down boy! Cut that shit out! Stop being so fucking greedy for Ashley's pussy, you stupid dick!

Doesn't work. I tried, right? Gave it my best shot. What more can I do?

She gapes at me, her eyes staring at my crotch. Aw yeah, that's right, Princess. Stroke my ego. I love it.

"What's with the towel?" I say, lifting one brow.

She snaps her eyes back to my face and blushes. "Um, I'm cold."

"You're not cold," I tell her. "It's like eighty degrees out, Princess. Ditch the towel and let's go for a swim."

She's clinging to that towel like it's her entire life. I don't even understand why. It's not like I haven't seen her naked before. We're just going swimming. What the fuck?

But, yeah, this shit happens. I've dealt with it before. It's cute when Ashley does it. Don't ask me why, it just is. I walk towards her and toss my own towel onto one of the pool lounge chairs, then reach for her and hers. She loosens her grip, and I pull her hand away slowly, taking the towel from her. Once we're done with that, I toss her towel into a chair, too.

"Come on," I say. "It's just swimming. Let's have some fun."

"Um..." she mumbles.

I lead her towards the steps heading into the shallow end, then help her down onto the first one. The water is warm and nice. Fuck, I love heated pools, you don't even know. Best invention ever. Nothing against cold water, but it can go suck a dick as far as I'm concerned.

I leave her at the steps into the shallow end and she panics.

"Where are you going?" she asks.

"Diving board?" I say.

"Oh."

She watches me the entire way there, still standing on the first step. It's her ankles. Just her ankles. She is up to her ankles in the water, and I don't know about you but I wouldn't consider that swimming. Don't worry, I'll fix this. I know exactly what to do.

I march up to the diving board, which probably looks comical. Yeah, my erection, remember? I don't give a fuck. I step out to the edge of the board and bounce a little. Intentionally. She's still watching me, and each time I bounce up and down, my cock does a little dance for her. I make a show of it, spinning a little. Helicopter or some shit? I don't know. She smiles and laughs, though.

After that, I dive in. A real dive, not some stupid boring jump. I know swimming, alright? I grew up with this pool. This isn't my first rodeo. I got this. There's barely a splash as I enter the water, and I sink down to the bottom of the pool easily. I stay low, swimming towards her, eyes latching onto her toes twinkling in the water.

Pink. She's got pink toenail polish on. I like it. It's cute. Matches her personality.

Her toes twitch when I get closer. I'm at the stairs now. I come above the surface, jumping up and rebounding off the bottom step of the stairs, then I grab her around the waist. She squeals and screams, kicking and flailing, but I fling her over my shoulder anyways. And that's what we do, that's how we enter the pool. She pounds on my back and screams at me while I carry her further and further into the pool.

"Ethan! Ethan, put me down! What are you--"

"Hold your breath, Princess," I say, laughing.

She's not going to. I know she won't. I'm not that much of a dick, though. I clap my hand over her mouth and nose to keep her from inhaling water, then I dunk us both down. Once we're under, she stops smacking my back. I shift and swim around so I'm facing her. She's holding her breath on her own now.

I used to play this game when I was a kid. Not sure if it's as exciting when you're older, but I want to play it with her now. I don't even know if you'd call it a game, but that's fine. I don't care.

I grin at her and sneak closer. Then, while we're both underwater, I kiss her.

She blinks, confused at first, but then she kisses me back. It's nothing too crazy. We're both underwater, remember? But it's fun and playful and flirty, and we keep kissing until we slowly float back to the surface. I duck away from her and start treading water. She does the same.

"What was that for?" she asks.

"What the fuck? I need a reason to kiss you?" I ask.

"Are you trying to seduce me, Ethan Colton?" she asks, glaring a little, smiling a little more. I love that flirty accusing tone in her voice. Sexy as fuck, that's what that is.

"Nah, just having fun with you, Princess. That alright?"

She bites her bottom lip and turns away. Her cheeks are red. I love that, too.

"I wish we could do more," she says. "I think it would be fun. I really am sore, though. I'm sorry."

"Hey," I say, swimming close to her. I put my hands on her hips and spin her so she's looking right at me. "Don't be sorry. Nothing to apologize for."

"Are you sure?" she asks. "You're not upset or disappointed or anything?"

"Nah, I'm not," I tell her. I'm not, either. I mean, shit, I'd love to fuck her right here and now, but there's more to life than sex, you know? Shut the fuck up. Don't judge me.

"I always feel weird swimming," she says. "Do you think I'm pretty?"

"What the fuck kind of question is that?"

She shrugs, which nearly sends her underwater. I pull her up before she goes too low, and she laughs.

"You're so weird," she says.

"I'm the weird one? You're the one asking if you're pretty."

"Well, how should I know if I'm pretty?"

"You're pretty," I say. "Trust me."

"How pretty?" she asks.

Are we really having this conversation? "Pretty as fuck," I say.

She laughs at me. "That doesn't help! Give me a number. From one to ten. Ten is the best."

"Twelve," I say.

"That's not between one and ten!"

"You think I fucking care?"

She laughs again. We're having a serious conversation here! I can't believe she's laughing at me.

God, she's beautiful. I love it when she smiles.

"Want to race?" she asks.

"You're asking me to race?" I ask. "You realize this is my pool? I've been swimming here since I was three. You think you can win?"

She makes a face at me, pursed lips, wrinkled nose, wide eyes. It's cute and arrogant all at once.

"Do *you* think you can win?" she asks me, trying not to smile.

"Whoa, you did not just say that," I say. "You don't want to bring out my competitive spirit, Princess."

"I'll bet you," she says. "I bet you I can win."

"What are the stakes?" I ask. "What do you get if you win?"

"Um... if I win, you have to make me lunch. I want a turkey club sandwich, with extra mayo."

"Shit, that's harsh. You're bringing your A game, I see."

"How about you?" she asks. "What do you want if you win?"

Her eyes sparkle. I can see it. I know what she's thinking. What do I want? I want to fuck that sweet pussy of yours, Princess.

But, nah. She's sore, remember? We have to lay off that. Give it a break. Also, what the fuck, if she gets a sandwich, I want something good, too. Sex is great, but we'll get to that later. Right now I want...

"If I win, I want you to make me one of those fruit smoothies you make sometimes."

"With the strawberries and bananas?" she asks, her ears perking up.

"Yeah, that. Those are great."

"It's not that exciting..." she says, but she smiles and blushes, too. Man, I will never be able to get enough of her red cheeks.

"Don't underestimate yourself," I tell her. "They're really good."

"Alright, well I'll make you one if you win," she says. "*If* you win, but..."

"Oh, there you go again, Princess. Keep it up. I'll go harder than hard. I'm not a good sport. I play to win."

She laughs and swims close to me, then hugs me. It's... I don't know. Unexpected? I don't care. I put my arms around her and hug her, too.

Yeah, we're naked. So what? Yeah, my cock is hard and pressed between her thighs. Does it look like I give a fuck? We're swimming here. We're racing. Serious shit is on the line. If I win I get a goddamn fruit smoothie. I've never wanted anything more in my entire life.

Maybe. Maybe not. They're really good, though. You should try one sometime.

Mia Clark

3 - Ashley

WE RACE AND ETHAN WINS. I knew he would win, but it was fun to race against him, still. I liked it, and I liked the way he favored me, like it was a serious and important competition. It's just silly, but I like how he's silly, too.

I think there's something wrong with me. I think I'm doing something wrong. This is supposed to be... we're um... with benefits, right? For a week, but...

No, stop that, Ashley.

We can still be friends after. We can still swim and race and make bets about lunch. Right? I hope so.

Can we swim naked, though? We're not having sex, so maybe it's fine? I'm not sure. I doubt it.

We play some more games, and then just swim around the pool. I challenge him to a breath holding competition, which he also wins, but it's close! I think it is. Maybe he just made it look like it's close by coming up right after I did, but I don't mind. It's still fun.

When we play Marco Polo, it's kind of strange, but interesting. Obviously we're the only ones in the pool, so we're just chasing each other, but we're also naked, so grabbing to tag the other person is... um...

Well, let's just say that Ethan ends up with more than a few handfuls of my breasts and once when I tagged him I accidentally grabbed him by the penis. I don't know how that happened. I think he did it on purpose, because when I opened my eyes to gloat, he just stood there, smirking at me until I realized I had my fingers wrapped around his cock.

When I blushed, he laughed even more.

It's still fun, though. We splash and enjoy ourselves and we're naked, but who cares? No one can see us. The pool is surrounded by a high fence, and it's just us here right now.

When we get out of the pool, we lay in our chairs on top of towels, letting the sun dry us off. I close my eyes and bask in the warmth. My fingers tingle and I reach over to where Ethan is, touching the armrest of his lounge chair. He sees me and taps his fingers against the back of my hand, then lifts my hand up and puts it in his. We hold hands like that, eyes closed, drying off. Our hands swing back and forth between us in the air, casual and sweet.

I didn't know that Ethan could be sweet before all of this.

I wonder if he's always been this way, or if...

No, stop it. Cut it out. He's not changing. He's still the same, you're just seeing a different side of him than before. That's what I tell myself, but I don't know if it's true.

"Hey," Ethan says, squeezing my fingers in his. "You hungry?"

"Yes," I say. As if on cue, my stomach grumbles.

"I know I won, but I've got a proposition for you," he says. "What do you say?"

I blink open one eye and regard him with suspicion. *A proposition?* "What is it?" I ask.

"I'll make us turkey clubs if you make us fruit smoothies. Deal?"

"Oooh, for lunch?" I ask. I hadn't thought about that, but they would go good together, wouldn't they?

"Yeah," he says. "Sound good?"

"Alright," I say.

Ethan stands up and takes his towel with him. I follow after him.

"Towel," he reminds me, pointing back to my chair.

"Oh, whoops!"

"Might want to wrap up," Ethan says. "It's cooler inside. Let's put some clothes on before lunch?"

I nod and start to wrap my towel around my body. Ethan heads to the door to let us back inside. He can't see me now, and I have an idea. This is either the best idea or the weirdest idea, but it's my idea and I'm going to do it.

I wrap my towel around just my waist, keeping my upper body and my breasts exposed. It's cooler inside, right? I rush up behind Ethan and slip through the door before him, hurrying in. And... yup! It's much cooler here. My nipples harden almost immediately, stiff and responsive.

I spin around quick before Ethan can come in. He stands there, mouth open and about to say something, but then he stops. His eyes snap down to my breasts and my nipples. He stares, and a slow grin creeps across his face.

"Now you're just teasing me, Princess," he says, grinning.

"I know," I say. "What do you think?"

"Your nipples look cold," he says. "Here, let me help you with that."

Help me with...?

He darts inside and grabs me by the waist, pinning me to the wall. Then he ducks low and wraps his lips around one of my nipples, sucking it into his mouth. Cool chill meets wet warmth. My nipple softens from the lack of cold air surrounding it, then hardens again from the sudden sensation. I gasp and forget to keep a hold on my towel. It drops to the floor just as my hands reach for the back of Ethan's head.

He keeps sucking on my nipple for a few more seconds, but it seems like an eternity. *Oh*, a wonderful eternity, though. When he pulls away, my fingers are still twined tight in his hair and I try to pull him back. He manages to sneak himself away from me, though.

"There," he says. "I warmed one of them up. Not sure if it helped, though."

"I think it helped," I say, dazed. "What about the other one?"

"Wow, you're greedy, huh?" he asks with a smirk.

"No!" I say, sticking my tongue out at him. "It just makes sense to do both!"

"Go put some clothes on, you greedy tease," he says.

I make a funny face at him, but he just laughs.

"Fine," I say, indignant, stomping one foot. "You too, though."

"Yeah, I probably should. Don't want my cock getting cold, do I? It might need some warming up."

I roll my eyes at him. "Oh, you'd like that, wouldn't you?"

"You're damn right I would."

I huff at him, but I smile, too. I really am cold now, and shivering, so I spin around to run up the stairs to get my clothes, but Ethan stops me with a hand around my stomach. He pulls me back, then slaps my butt hard. The smack echoes through the room, and I jolt and jump in surprise. It didn't hurt, but...

Well, it didn't hurt, and it kind of felt nice? I wouldn't mind him doing it again...

"Towel!" he says. "You just going to leave it laying on the floor or what?"

I spin back to him, glaring. "You just wanted an excuse to spank me, didn't you?"

"Yeah, actually, I did," he says. "Not that I need one."

"Maybe I didn't like it!" I tell him.

"What rule was it that there's no lying?" he asks.

"Seven," I say, muttering.

"I'm invoking rule number seven. You liked when I smacked your ass, didn't you?"

"Maybe."

"Good," he says. "Because, yeah, you've got the most smackable ass I've ever seen, Princess. I just want to fucking--" And he turns me around and spanks me again!

Wow. Really? Yes, really. Wow?

Ethan pulls me back to him and hugs me tight. He's warm, or we're warm together, and it's nice. He kisses me on the cheek, then whispers in my ear. "I'm just playing with you. You know that, right, Ashley? If you want me to cut it out, just say it."

"Princess!" I hiss at him.

"Whoa, holy fuck, what, do you not even have a name now?"

"Princess Ashley?" I ask.

"I think you're getting a little carried away with yourself here."

"Please?"

He rolls his eyes. "Yeah, whatever. *Princess Ashley.* You good?"

"Mhm," I say, slipping in to kiss him quick. On the lips. Just once.

"You better go upstairs and get dressed before I forget you're sore," he growls.

"I was *going,*" I say, "but *someone* just *had* to stop me and smack my smackable ass."

"Damn right!" he says.

I bend down to grab my towel and he spanks me again. Afterwards, Ethan swaggers off, towel draped over his shoulder, his erection bouncing proud in front of him, and he heads upstairs.

Well, good. Good! I do need clothes. I'm getting cold. A little. I kind of wonder what it would be like to warm up beneath his blankets, though. With him on top of me. And inside me. Kissing me. Holding me.

Later! Tomorrow. Tonight? I don't know. *Soon.*

I wonder if aspirin helps get rid of sex soreness? I should find out.

4 - Ethan

W E MAKE OUR FOOD, then eat it while cuddling on the couch and watching some TV show. Did I ever tell you how cuddly this girl is? Cuddly as fuck, that's what she is. It's cute, though. She starts to shiver a little since she's wearing these short shorts, so I grab a blanket from the back of the couch and cover us in it.

"Next time wear pants," I tell her.

She pouts at me and wrinkles her nose. "No. I don't want to."

"Wow, fine. Suit yourself. I was just looking out for you."

"Keep me warm," she says.

Whoa, demanding much? I stare at her, and she tries to match me, stare for stare. Oh shit, a competition? Yeah, I don't back down, Princess.

Eventually she blinks. I probably blinked too. Oh well. What can you do?

I pull her close and wrap the blankets tight around us while we eat. It's good. Everything is good. All of this is really fucking good. Not the TV show. I don't even know what the fuck is happening with that. It's just white noise in the background, something to do.

"What do you want to do after this?" she asks.

I shrug. "Didn't have any plans."

"What would you have done if we weren't hanging out?"

Huh. What would I have done? Takes me a second, but then I remember.

"Probably lifted weights. I don't want to get lazy this summer. Need to keep in shape, you know?"

"Alright," she says.

"Alright what?"

"You can go lift weights."

"And you'll..." I'm not following where she's going with this.

"Can I watch?" she asks. "We can talk or something?"

This isn't exactly the first time I've had girls want to watch me working out, but I feel like she's asking for a different reason. I'm pretty sure she just wants to hang out and talk, not watch my rippling biceps and tight abs. To be fair, if I'm lifting alone, she probably won't see all that much of that, anyways. Need a spotter to do any real heavy lifting, so I'll just be doing average stuff. Doesn't matter to me. It's just to keep in the habit.

"Yeah," I say. "I guess?"

"Do you not want me to watch?" she asks.

"Might be boring," I say.

"I think it will be fun," she says.

I shrug. "Alright."

When we finish up eating, we head to the weight room. It's nothing too crazy here, not like a regular gym, but it's got everything I need. Bench press, some dumbbells, a pull up station, Roman chair, ab station, the whole nine yards. Oh, and a treadmill. Can't forget cardio, now can we?

I set up my stuff while she sits on a spare bench, watching me.

5 - *Ashley*

'VE ALWAYS KNOWN ETHAN WORKED OUT. I knew it in high school, and I knew it when our parents got married, but I've never actually seen him do it. He gets this intense look on his face as he works his muscles. It's a deep concentration, never faltering, completely focused. I watch him move through each motion, step by step. His muscles ripple and strain, but I like the look on his face the most.

It's almost zen-like, as if this is his way of meditating. I can't even imagine Ethan meditating, though. I couldn't have before now, but now I can. It's interesting and different.

"Why did you quit?" he asks me.

"What?"

"Cheerleading. Why'd you quit?"

"I was never on the cheerleading squad," I say, but I don't think that's the answer he wants.

"When we were freshman in high school, I saw you trying out. You went to the first day of practice, but then you never came back. Why not?"

"I don't know," I say. I do know, but I'd forgotten all about that until now. I'd forgotten the reason I wanted to be a cheerleader in the first place.

"You sure?" he asks.

He could tell me we're following the rules if he wants. Rule number seven. He could, but he doesn't.

"I was embarrassed," I say.

"What? Why?"

"I..." I hesitate for a second, but then I decide to tell him. I want to tell him. "I was the only girl with glasses," I say. "I don't know if they were telling the truth. Now that I know better, I don't think they were. The head cheerleader and her second told me that girls with glasses are ugly, though. I could still try out for the team, but I couldn't wear my glasses, not even during practice."

"That's bullshit," Ethan says. He finishes his current lift, benchpressing, and slams the bar back into its holder. "They seriously told you that? There was a girl with glasses once, though."

"Yeah," I say. "Later, but not when I tried out. I thought they were telling the truth."

I thought they were telling the truth about everything. That I couldn't be a cheerleader with glasses and that girls with glasses were ugly...

"Is that why the... LASIK?" Ethan asks.

"Your dad didn't have to do that," I say. "I wasn't even going to ask. I didn't. My mom asked him about it later."

"I liked your glasses. I like you without glasses, too. Whatever works for you."

That's... my heart swells. No one's ever said something like that to me before. None of the boys I've dated knew me before when I had glasses. I always wondered if they'd still want to go out with me if I still had them, too. It was a weird secret to keep, and I know I shouldn't be ashamed about it. Plenty of people have glasses, right? I was, though. I was embarrassed and scared, and...

"Do you like girls with glasses?" I ask him.

He gives me a funny look. "Huh?"

"Um... I mean, do you think girls with glasses can be attractive? I've always wondered about that."

"You've always wondered if *I* think girls with glasses can be attractive?" Ethan asks, dubious.

"Not you!" Well, no, that's not entirely true, now is it...? "Just boys in general, I mean."

"Yeah," he says. "Depends on the girl, but yeah. You looked nice in them."

"Thanks," I say, looking away, trying to hide my blush. I don't know why I'm blushing around him so much lately. It's weird.

Ethan gets up and heads to the pull up station. It's some giant monstrosity of metal and different levels of bars, for all different types of pull ups, chin ups, and more. I'm not entirely sure what's what with it. It's the first time I've ever seen some-one use it.

"How did you remember me trying out to be a cheerleader?" I ask him. "I didn't think you would have noticed."

His shoulders stiffen. Maybe. He shrugs. Were they stiff because of him shrugging? I don't think so, but it's hard to tell.

"I remember lots of shit," he says.

Oh, really? Well, I remember wanting to try out for the cheerleader squad because I knew he was going to play football. It was stupid, though. He never would have noticed me. That's what I thought. He did notice me, though. Not in the way I thought he might. I don't even know what I was thinking, because Ethan Colton's always been a troublemaker and a bad boy, and I was being more than stupid.

I had some dreamy vision of what might happen, though. Maybe his team won the game. I don't even know how football works. There's a ball and sides and throwing and running. Ethan was the quarterback. He's still the quarterback in college; I asked my mom about it once and she told me, but I told her not to tell him I asked.

In my dream, his team won, and when we were celebrating victory, in the spur of the moment he came over and kissed me. Since I was a cheerleader then, in my dream, I was a lot more athletic, and I jumped in his arms or something and... I don't remember. It involved a lot of kissing and athleticism and maybe more.

I did like the idea of more. I kind of still like the idea of more. We're doing more right now, aren't we?

For a week, at least. That's it.

"I liked cheerleading," I tell him. "I know I didn't really do it a lot. Just that one day. I liked it, though. I was just scared after. I know it's stupid. My mom almost called the school to complain, but I begged her not to."

"You should have told me," he says. "I would have set the record straight with this prissy stuck up bitches."

I laugh and roll my eyes at him. "You weren't even my stepbrother then, Ethan."

"So?" he says, like it's a challenge and he dares me to doubt him.

"You wouldn't have even cared," I say, trying to act nonchalant.

"Fuck you, I cared," he says.

Maybe he did. He noticed me trying out for the squad, didn't he? It's too late now, though.

He finishes his pull ups and hops down to the ground, then turns and smiles at me. "I should probably go easy today. Don't want to get too worked up."

"Huh?" I ask. "What's that mean?"

"It's--" He stops himself and furrows his brow, biting his cheek. "You want to know?"

"Sure?" I don't get it.

"After a real intense workout, testosterone and shit kind of screws with your mind. Makes you horny as hell and ready to fuck."

"What? No way! Is that real?" I... I don't know if I believe him, but I can't figure out what his angle is if he's lying to me.

"Hey, I don't lie about this shit, Princess. All I know is the harder I work out, the more I want to fuck after. You're sore, so that shit's not going to work."

"Oh," I say.

"Yeah, that's right."

"Well, if you're gentle..."

He pauses. He was about to go grab some dumbbells, but he stops and turns back towards me.

"What's that supposed to mean?"

"I'm still sore, but if you go gentle, I think it would be alright?"

"Gentle?" he asks. "Gentle is alright?"

"I mean *really* gentle, Ethan."

"Hey," he says. "What about the hot tub?"

"Um... what?"

"Look, I can do gentle, Princess. I'm just saying that what if we go in the hot tub, too? Help relax with some water and heat. It'll keep everything slippery and smooth, too. Gentle and relaxing as fuck."

"In the hot tub?" I ask. "Sex?"

"Listen, you're the one that brought it up. Should I start lifting hard or what?"

Oh. Huh. Um.

"Well, you can if you want to..." My cheeks are red. I know this, but I don't look away this time. I try not to. I find myself looking down at his chin, but then I make myself look him in the eyes.

"If you change your mind, I can just take care of myself. You let me know, alright?"

"If you do that, can I watch?" I ask.

"Holy fuck, you're freaky as hell, aren't you?" Ethan asks, grinning.

"No! I just... I was just asking!"

"Yeah, you can watch, Princess. Whatever you want."

"Alright," I say. "Then, yes. I would like if you lifted more."

"You know by saying that you're basically telling me you want me to get hard?"

"You're going to be hard anyways," I counter.

"Whoa, tough girl now, huh? Little Miss Perfect learns how to give a blowjob and now she thinks she's all that?"

I cross my hands over my chest, just under my breasts, and huff at him. "I'm just stating the obvious."

"Yeah, you keep it up, Smarty Pants. Let's see how that goes."

I think I will! I want to see how it goes...

Mia Clark

6 - Ethan

THIS ISN'T HOW I planned to spend my night. I'm not even sure what we're doing, but it's kind of fun in a fucked up sort of way. Here, let me lay it out for you quick.

Hot tub.

Me.

Ashley.

We're naked.

Sexy shit is about to go down.

That's all you really have to know. You want more? Well, fuck, aren't you greedy?

"Alright, go slow," she says.

"I'm not even in yet," I tell her. "We haven't started. How can I go slow?"

"Go slow when you start!" she says, laughing.

"What the fuck, are you sassing me?" I ask, smirking at her.

"No," she says. "Yes."

"Make up your mind, Princess. Which is it?"

"No-yes."

"Real fucking cute," I say. "Alright, uh... lean back? I'll be gentle."

Gentle? Yeah, that's what I said. I'm going to be gentle with her. It's cool. I can handle it. Delicate fucking Princess Ashley. Nah, for real, though, she's sore and I don't want to be a dick about that. It happens. Usually I wouldn't be doing this, and I'd just give her a break for the day, but she's the one that started it. This isn't my fault, it's hers.

Yeah, I made her sore in the first place, but she's the one that told me I could lift hard and get worked up, and now she's dealing with the consequences. You can't do that to someone. It's just rude.

"Like this?" she asks.

Holy fuck. Yeah... just like that...

She leans backwards, the middle of her back pressed against the edge of the hot tub. With her body arched like that, her breasts look massive against her petite frame, and her taut stomach is gorgeous as fuck. I run my hand from her hips, up her stomach, to her breasts, admiring the view and groping her.

Gently, of course. No fucking idea why I'm being gentle with her breasts, because it's her pussy that's overworked, but whatever. There needs to be comparable interaction. I think that's some physics rule. Newton's third law? A body set in motion stays in motion? I don't fucking know. I'll put her in motion alright, that's for sure.

"Ethan, what are you--"

"Playing with your breasts," I say, interrupting her. I interrupt her even more with my lips pressed against hers, kissing her. "Quiet, Princess. Let's do this."

"I like the water," she says. "You were right. It's warm and relaxing. I do feel a little better."

"You ready, then?" I ask.

Even though I asked her, I reach between her legs and check for myself, too. I lean closer to her, my body pressed tight to hers, my hard abs to her soft stomach. I stroke two fingers up and down her slit, then slowly, gentle as fuck, push inside of her. She bucks her hips up to meet me, then hisses.

"Please, slow, slow slow slow."

"Shit, it's just my fingers," I say. "Are you sure you want to do this? We don't have to. We can go... go fucking cuddle or something?"

Cuddle? Did I seriously just suggest we go cuddle instead of having sex? Who the fuck am I and what have I done with Ethan? I'm having an identity crisis or an existential crisis or some kind of crisis. Probably more than one. What's the plural of crisis? Crises?

Might as well ask Ashley. She's the smart one.

"Hey," I say. "What's more than one crisis called?"

She snaps open her eyes and stares at me. "What?"

I pull my fingers out and wrap my hand around my cock, guiding it towards her entrance.

"You know, like if you're dealing with a crisis, but there's two of them, what's that called?"

"A catastrophe?" she offers. "What do you mean? Like an earthquake and a tornado?"

"No, not a different word. The same word, but more than one."

"Plural?"

I move closer to her. My cock is on a mission, ready to go deep undercover. This is serious espionage shit, covert stealth operative. I need to penetrate her pussy's defenses and leave my seed behind as a marker. I don't know where I come up with this shit. I might be screwed up.

"I... um... I don't know?" she says. "Crises..." Her eyes widen and she stops suddenly. "Slow!"

"Holy fuck it's just the head!" I say to her.

"Ethan, please!"

That's it. I'm in. Sort of. Just the tip. The head of my cock is most decidedly lodged inside of her pussy, but there's a whole fucking lot more to go, and I'm just standing here, surrounded by hot water and bubbles and this beautiful girl's body beneath me, my gorgeous fucking Princess, and that's it. I can't move. I stay still and wait.

"Alright, you can go a little--"

I shift slightly and push forward, but she stops me before I even start. Her hands crash against my chest and she holds me at bay.

"Listen, I'm going slow as fuck," I tell her. "We're not going to get anywhere like this. Why don't we just stop?"

Yeah, I'm telling her we should stop. *Fuck me.* I can't deal with this. My cock is hard as fuck and I just want to sink inside her golden pussy and feel her pulse and press against my shaft, but it's not going to work. Anyone can see this, except for Ashley.

"No, we can do it," she says. "I'll stop, I won't say anything. You can keep going."

I push a little more in. Just barely. A fraction of a quarter of an inch. Slow. Very slow. Gentle and soft and slow and I even squeeze her breast and tease her nipple and kiss her to take her mind off of it, but the way she clenches her eyes shut, wincing, makes me stop. I stand there, staring at her, my lips touching hers, my hand cupping her breast.

"What?" she asks me after awhile, opening her eyes.

"How many times have you had sex?" I ask.

"I don't know. A few?"

"Ashley, how many times is a few?"

"Why did you call me Ashley?"

"This is a serious conversation," I tell her. "We need to be serious right now."

"Um... well... I think five? Five times? Maybe four."

"How the fuck does that work?" I ask her. "We've had sex more than that already."

I don't actually know if we've had sex more than that. I haven't been counting, I've just been enjoying myself.

"I meant before you and I um... before we did. It was four or five times. It might have been three," she says. She does that thing where she starts counting in her mind, eyes narrowed, looking slightly up at numbers that only exist in her thoughts.

"So what you're saying," I say, "is that you're basically a virgin."

"I'm not a virgin, Ethan Colton!"

"Whoa, full names. Shit, I struck a chord, huh?"

"Shut up. Are you going to fuck me now or what?"

"I'm fucking trying!" Wait, hold up. Did she just...? "Did you just swear? Holy shit."

"I did not," she says, blushing and looking away from me.

"I heard you, Princess. Don't lie to me."

"It wasn't a swear word," she says. "It was a verb. An action that needs doing."

"You're going to try to beat me on a technicality? I'm not sure that's how this works."

While we're talking, arguing about whether she swore or simply used a verb, I push in a little more. Barely anything at all. I do it when she doesn't notice, when she's thinking and scrunching up her brow, trying to make a point. It's cute as fuck, and it works in my favor.

Seriously, though, only three times? Maybe five. What the fuck was that stupid ass boyfriend of hers doing? Ex-boyfriend now. Yeah, she's not getting back together with him. You know why? If he tries, I'll beat the fuck out of him.

I kind of want to do that to every guy that even looks at her with lust in his eyes. Is that wrong? I think it's my duty as her stepbrother to protect her like that, so it's probably fine, except how am I supposed to protect her from me? Kick my own ass? Easier not to think about it.

"Alright, maybe I swore--" she says. "Oh my God, you're in."

I smirk. Damn right I am!

It's a little weird, because I think it took me something like five minutes just to get all the way inside her, but now that I am, I feel accomplished. My cock twitches at the thought of it, at the idea of a successful mission, except now what the fuck do I do? Pull out and then spend five more minutes going back? Fucking hell...

"It feels nice," she says, wrapping her arms around me and purring into my ear. "I like you inside me, Ethan."

"Me, too," I say. "I think we have a problem, though."

"What?"

"How am I supposed to pull out and thrust back in? This is going to take forever, Princess."

"Oh. Yeah... um..."

"I've got an idea."

"What is it?"

I take one of her hands and guide it towards her pussy. I pull out two of her fingers, pressing them together, then I lay them on her clit. I have to lean back a little and give her some room at first, but it's not so bad. I'm still inside her and that's what counts.

"Play with yourself," I tell her. "I'll just stay in. That work?"

"You... you want me to masturbate?" she asks.

"Yeah, why not?"

"I thought we were having sex?" she says.

"Sometimes you need to improvise a little," I tell her. "I'll stay in and bask in the delicious fucking warm tightness of your pussy, and you tease your clit and work yourself up. When you cum, you'll squeeze against my cock. It'll work."

I'll be doing other shit, too. Like kissing her, groping her breasts, and just having an all-around good time. Maybe some gentle rocking back and forth for a little motion. We'll see how it goes.

"I... alright," she says.

"Don't tell me you've never masturbated before?" I say.

"I have!" she practically shouts.

It's so absurd I laugh. My Princess has some real masturbatory pride over here, don't you forget it!

She looks at me funny and then I realize what's wrong. Not too hard to figure out.

"It's sexy as hell," I tell her. "I want you to enjoy yourself, Princess. You want to know what sex is? It's not anything. It's whatever the hell you want it to be. As long as we're both having fun and enjoying ourselves, then that's it. It doesn't have to be all thrusting and fucking, hard and crazy shit, alright? Right now we're going to have sex like this, and it'll still be great."

"Are you sure?" she asks. "I just... I've masturbated before, Ethan, but never during sex. I didn't think I was supposed to."

"Who the fuck told you not to?" I ask.

She shrugs and teases her clit a little. I can feel her hand pressed between my stomach and hers. "I thought guys wouldn't like it, because they'd think they weren't good enough?"

"Obviously they aren't good enough," I tell her. "You said you'd never had an orgasm during sex before me. You should have fucking told them they were shit."

She laughs. She full on laughs. It's loud and silly and giddy and fun. It's a little weird because I'm balls deep inside of her while we're both naked in the hot tub and her fingers are on her clit, but it's cool. Whatever works, right?

"You're so strange," she says.

"Listen, Princess, I'm going to tell this to you straight. If you don't like something, you just tell the stupid fuck that you don't like it, alright? Promise me."

She sticks out her tongue at me. I have an urge to suck it into my mouth and kiss the fuck out of her, but I restrain for a second.

"I can't do that," she says. "It'd be mean."

"What rule are we up to?" I ask her. "Also, keep playing with your clit."

"We're talking, though," she says.

"Do I look like I give a fuck? We can talk and have sex at the same time. Holy shit."

She laughs again, but she starts teasing and toying with her clit, too. I can feel her pressing slightly against me and my cock tightens and throbs in response.

"Yeah, just like that, Princess. Feel good?"

"Mhm," she says, nodding. "We're on fourteen."

"Glad you're keeping track. I'd be fucked without you."

"No," she says, making a silly face at me. "You are with me."

"Whoa, Princess has jokes, huh?" I laugh. "I have to admit, that was pretty good."

"Thank you for doing this with me," she says, soft. "I like it a lot. I just... I'm sore but we only have a week and..."

I kiss her quick. She kisses me back. Her eyes flutter shut and I close mine, too, giving in to the passion. This isn't lust right now. I don't know what the fuck it is. We're definitely not fucking. Kind of making love, I guess? Gentle and soft as fuck, and there's no real movement besides what's going on inside her and what's happening with her hands. It's different and I can't say I ever expected to do something like this, but I really like it, too.

"Princess," I whisper to her. "I want to make another rule. Rule number fourteen. I know it's going to sound fucked up, but I want you to agree to it, alright?"

She nods and keeps teasing herself, keeping her eyes closed. "A-alright..."

"Feels good, huh?" I ask. I rock slightly, moving my cock a little, but trying to be careful with her. Gentle.

"Y-yes..."

"You keep doing that and just listen, then," I say. "Rule number fourteen is that I don't want you to put up with stupid shit from stupid guys. Yeah, the rest of these rules are supposed to be for a week or whatever the fuck, but I want this one to be for forever. If they suck in bed, you tell them, or you play with yourself, and if they get mad and try to yell at you, you just tell me and I'll kick the shit out of them."

She starts to smile and laugh, but I kiss her to stop her. I just want her to concentrate right now. I want her to be happy. I want her to have an orgasm and enjoy herself and not have to put up with any stupid shit.

She nods slightly. "I... I'm getting close, I think," she says.

Yeah, I can feel it. My cock swells, and I rock inside her, just small gentle motions, like an ocean wave or something. The warmth and the bubbles from the hot tub surround us, too. This is zen. We are Buddhist monks, at one with ourselves and the universe. If orgasms aren't the meaning of life and existence, I don't know what is. We're just two people trying to find our spiritual nirvana. Something like that. I don't know anything about Buddhism, so don't go getting all fucking uptight if I screwed that up.

"Ethan..." she says. "Um... can I talk to you about stuff like that? Later, I mean? Like um... can I call you and talk to you on the phone when we're back at college?"

It's weird, because, yeah, I have her phone number, but I don't think I've ever texted her or called her. She's texted me a few times, but just to tell me small stuff like what we're having for dinner or that dinner would be ready soon. Things like that, you know? Not real conversations, just dumb family junk.

We've talked. I guess. I don't know if I'd consider it that. This is more, though.

"I don't know if I can have conversations with you about guys fucking you," I tell her. I feel like I should be honest about that one.

"Please?" she asks.

Holy fuck, why is she asking me this now? Her eyes are scrunched up and I can feel her, inside and out. Her breathing is getting heavier and her stomach is tightening and flexing. Her breasts sway side to side a little, her arm shaking, hand and fingers teasing at her clit. She clenches against my cock like a glove, grabbing and holding me inside her.

She's about to have an orgasm and she's asking me to agree to talk to her about girl shit when she goes back to college.

The problem here is that her orgasm is goading me on, and yeah, I haven't moved a ton, but I'm going to cum soon, too. Real soon. I could probably do it now, but I'm holding off. I want to do it with her. Is that weird? I don't care if it is.

The sun is setting all around us. The sky is turning darker, purples and blues mixing with light orange and bright red and a hint of yellow. A sliver of the pale moon crests out in the sky to my left, and I can see a few bright stars finally making an appearance in the beginnings of the night sky. And it's me and her, Ashley, Little Miss Perfect, Goodie Two Shoes, Smarty Pants, Princess.

I don't want to admit it, but this is romantic. Everything about what we're doing is romantic, and it's kind of fucked up because this is my sister. No, fuck you, my stepsister. And it's not fucked up. I love it. It's really nice, and I'm enjoying myself, and the look on her face says she's enjoying herself, too.

She speeds up a little, teasing and caressing her clit faster. This is it. We're going. Lost and gone. Over the edge. Heading from sunset to nightfall, and there's not a fucking thing either of us can do about it.

"Please?" she asks again, begging, whimpering.

I kiss her soft and she opens her mouth for me. I tease my tongue out and dance with hers, slow and sweet.

"Yeah," I tell her. "Alright."

That's it. It's like I've given her permission to orgasm. Not exactly, and it takes a few more moments, but soon enough she's good to go. She shivers and squirms beneath me, but I hold her in place, my hands on her hips. This isn't rough or hard, but it's powerful and strong. As soon as I feel the first tremors of her climax gripping at my cock, I lose it, too. My body tightens with hers and my balls squeeze and clench, shooting forth my cum. I fill her, deep and intense. I can't stop. I don't want to stop.

Our bodies dance like that, twisting and squirming, gentle and sweet, intense and hard. I kiss her, then I bite her bottom lip, pulling it into my mouth. She opens her mouth and lets out a gasp. Her hand moves from her clit to my back and she squeezes me tight against her. Rocking back and forth, delicate and calm, I help us both ride our orgasms towards something amazing and surreal.

It's darker now. When I open my eyes, the sun is fully set, but I'm still inside her, still holding her. The hot tub turns off on its own, leaving us in the wake of mutual pleasure and silence. The lights are on inside, though. It's not completely dark. I can see her face, see how she's looking at me, and...

It's both scary and awe-inspiring all at once. This is the kind of girl you see, that you *really* see. Once you see it, you can't unsee it, either. This is the kind of girl that you just want to fall in love with. Over and over. And, yeah, I realize how fucked up it is for me to say that, but it's the truth.

It's not like... shit... it's not like I'm *going* to fall in love with her. I can't. But she's...

Just fuck it. I don't have to explain this to you.

We kiss some more. It's gentle and cute, two lovers kissing during the aftermath of beautiful sexual exploration. I've never kissed someone like this before. She giggles and nips at my lip and I smirk and lick the tip of her nose, which makes her laugh some more. I try to pull out of her, but she clings tight to me, refusing to let me leave.

"No," she says.

"Yeah," I say. "I should probably stay inside you. Need to stretch you out and get you used to my cock. I'm kind of huge, so it'll work."

"You are pretty big," she says.

"Pretty big? That's it? Wow."

"You're bigger than everyone I've been with, but I haven't been with a lot!" she protests.

I shake my head side to side and sigh. "I can't believe I basically took your virginity."

She groans. "Shut up. You did not."

"Yeah, alright."

"How many girls have you been with?" she asks.

"Princess, let's not talk about that."

She pouts.

Well, what the fuck? Do you want to know something? A secret? Yeah, I'm not going to tell her this shit. It's not like I regret anything, but do you know how many girls I wish I'd been with?

I'm probably only saying this because I'm drunk off of her affection. It's more intoxicating than any alcohol I've ever had, and I feel like that's saying a lot since I'm a troublemaking bad boy, so...

I just kind of wish it was one. Just her. I wish I was as pure as her. I wish I wasn't a fucking prick and an arrogant asshole, because I feel like this would be a whole hell of a lot easier that way, but...

Yeah, that's not the answer. I honestly don't remember the answer, either. I actually do, but I don't want to tell you. Stop prying and being a nosy fuck.

The doorbell rings, interrupting us. We both hear it. It's not hard to hear. There's even a speaker outside so that you can hear it from the yard, which is where we currently are, in the hot tub by the pool.

"What's that?" she asks, stiffening.

"Shh, it's... look, it's not like before, alright? I ordered pizza. It's the pizza guy."

Not sure if you realize this, but I'm still inside her at this point and we're both naked and wet. Makes this whole situation kind of difficult.

"You ordered pizza before we had sex?" she asks, looking completely dumbfounded and con- fused.

"Listen, I thought we'd be done a hell of a lot sooner than this. I thought we'd be out and dressed and--"

The doorbell rings again.

"Well, fuck," I say.

"Go answer the door!" she says.

"Stop fucking clinging to me, then!"

She laughs and finally lets me go. I ease out of her, gentle, kissing her softly to keep her comfortable and safe. I don't fucking care if the pizza guy is at the gate. I'll answer him when I damn well please. Ashley's body is way more important than him.

I'm finally out and I step up and out of the tub, but she grabs my hand and stops me before I can toss on my pants.

"Kiss?" she asks.

I grin like a huge fucking idiot, which is probably what I am right now. Bending down, I give her a quick kiss before I go. The doorbell rings again. Can't this dude fucking wait a second?

I curse under my breath and pull my pants on, then run inside, grab the money I left on the dining room table, and head to the front door to get to the gate where this stupid fucking interloper is waiting.

The pizza better be good. Damn fucking good.

Spoilers: it is. Delicious as fuck.

Ashley and I cuddle on the couch and watch a movie while gorging on pizza. She put her pajamas on first, and begged me to get mine on, so I do. This is like some slumber party shit or something. It's kind of fun. I can't say I've ever screwed around and watched a movie with a girl three nights in a row, but I could get used to this.

We're even watching something I picked out. It's a fantasy movie with knights and magic and all sorts of high adventure craziness.

"Who's that?" she asks, nudging and nuzzling me. "Why are her ears like that?"

"She's an elf," I say. "She's the elf princess. That knight dude wants to fuck her hard, so he's going to go on a quest for her."

"She's like me," Ashley says.

"You're not an elf," I say.

"No, but I'm a princess."

"Damn fucking right you are."

"Are you my knight?" she asks.

"Yeah, I guess I am."

I feel like there's hidden meaning here, but I guess if the knight wants to fuck the princess hard, then yeah, that's what I am. Don't dig any deeper than that. Get the fuck away from me with your psychological bullshit.

When the movie's over and we're finished with our pizza, we creep upstairs. Ashley yawns and I tickle her slightly, which makes her start laughing and yawning at the same time. It's cute.

"Do you... want to sleep together again?" she asks.

"Yeah, sure," I say, squeezing her hand tight in mine.

"Can we sleep in my room tonight?" she asks. "Then we can sleep in your room tomorrow?"

"Whatever you want, Princess," I say, leaning in to kiss her quick.

She squeezes my hand and leads me down the hall to her bedroom. Belatedly, I realize I've never really been in here. I mean, yeah, I've been in here, but mostly just a step or two. Never for long. I've never spent time in her room with her, but now we're about to spend the entire night together. It's a weird thought, but comforting, too.

She pulls me in and closes the door behind her, then guides me to the bed in the dark. Lifting up the covers, she pushes me gently towards the bed until I sit then lay down. Quick, she jumps on top of me and rolls over me to her side of the bed, then sweeps the covers up and over us.

We lay like that in the dark, on our backs, wearing soft pajamas, staring at the ceiling.

"Can I sleep on you again tonight?" she asks. "I liked it last night. I just don't want you to think I'm weird."

"Make it a rule, then," I say, turning to look at her.

I see the faint glimmer of her smile in the darkness. "Alright. Rule number fifteen. We have to sleep together every night like this, and cuddle, too."

"Well, I guess I have to now," I say, pretending to grumble. "It's a rule."

"Do you want to, also, though?" she asks.

It takes me a second to think about it. Just a second. Not long.

"Yeah," I say. "I do. Come here, Princess."

7 - Ashley

ASHLEY? ETHAN?"

I'm tired. What time is it? What time did I go to bed? I blink open my eyes and look over to my bedside table to check the digital clock there. I know it's summer and I don't have anywhere to go, but still, it's ten o'clock which is kind of late for me. Usually I'm up a lot earlier.

Oh well. It doesn't really matter, right?

I hear her again. "Ashley, honey, are you here? Ethan?" It's my mom.

I hear Ethan's dad say something, but it's muffled and I can barely make it out. They're both downstairs. It sounds kind of like, "I'm sure they're fine. Sleeping in late or out doing something."

Yup, that's what I'm doing. Sleeping in late. I yawn and nuzzle up close to Ethan and cuddle under the blankets a little more before shouting out. "I'm up here, Mom!"

And that's when it hits me.

Ethan is awake now, too. We're both... oh my God, we're naked. Why are we naked? I could have sworn we went to sleep wearing pajamas, but something must have happened. I think back to the middle of the night, and then I remember. We didn't have sex, or not again at least, but we stripped down and played around for a little when we both ended up waking up at the same time. It was still dark and we were kissing and cuddling and it was a lot of fun, but now, um...

Now we're both naked in my bed and I can hear my mom coming up the stairs as we speak. This is *not* good.

"Fuck," Ethan says.

"Hide!" I whisper to him. "I thought you said they were going to be gone for a week?"

"That's what they told me," he says. "Where the fuck do you want me to hide?"

The bathroom? Under the bed? Um... hello! Anywhere but naked and right next to me would be really great, Ethan! And any of those places might work, but my mom is at my door right now, knocking, and I see the wiggle of the doorknob as she's about to open it, so...

I shove Ethan under the blankets and push him down so it looks kind of like there's just a lump there. That's what I hope, at least. I have some stuffed animals on the floor next to my bed that I sleep with sometimes, so I grab one quick and push it under the covers with its head showing so it kind of looks like maybe the lump is from stuffed animals? I hope. This isn't going to work, is it?

As a last ditch effort I lift my knees up slightly to give Ethan a little more hiding room. Sort of. I really hope this works. I know he's there, and when I look to my side all I can see is the slight shape of his body hiding under the covers, but my mom doesn't know he's there, and she has no reason to suspect he's here with me, and she especially has no reason to believe he'd be naked, that he would have slept with me, sex or otherwise, and...

She opens the door and peeks in at me.

"Hey there, sleepyhead," she says. "Having a late day today?"

I pretend to yawn and I nod at her. "I went to bed late," I say.

"That's alright. Sorry I couldn't be here when you got back. Did Ethan tell you? We came back as soon as we could. It turned out to be a shorter trip than we thought. Nothing too serious."

"Yup," I say. "He told me. I'm glad you're back."

I am. I know it's true when I say it, but some part of me rejects the answer, too. Am I really? I *am*, but I'm also not. What does this mean for us? Ethan and I?

It means we're done. I know it as soon as I think it, and I know it must be true. We can't keep up what we were doing, not with my mom and his dad back home. It's not like we can just swim naked whenever we want anymore. We can't have sex on the pool table. We can't cuddle and kiss randomly on the couch while watching TV and eating pizza.

I guess we could sneak around, but I'm not sure if that would work, either. We really shouldn't have done what we did at the drive-in movie theatre. Also, we can't go there every day, either. They play the same movies for a week or two, and it'd be suspicious. We might be able to sneak some time together alone upstairs in our rooms, but there'd always be the risk that someone would hear us, and we'd have to be quiet, and...

"Is everything alright, honey?" my mom asks.

I gulp. She knows, doesn't she? The look on her face looks like the look of someone who knows exactly what's going on, and she's trying to figure out what she thinks about it.

"Um..." Should I tell her? Just come clean? No! I can't do that. I can't.

"I thought you would have called me, that's all," she says. "I was wondering why you didn't. I thought maybe something was wrong. Are you sick? I can pick you up some soup at the store if you want."

I didn't even call my own mother. For nearly four days! If anything, that's the most suspicious thing of all. We talk almost every day, or more like every other day, but still. This isn't going to fly.

"Ethan said you two were probably busy, so I didn't want to bother you," I say. This is a lie. A huge lie. I'm lying to my mother and she's going to see through me immediately.

"That's true," she says. "I could have made some time for you. Sorry I didn't call you, either. Everything was just so hectic. When I finally had a chance to sit down for the day, it was always so late, and I didn't know if you'd be up or not. I guess I didn't have to worry about that if you've been going to bed late, though."

What would I have been doing if she called last night? Late? How late? I might have been having sex with Ethan in the hot tub. Or we might have been eating pizza and cuddling on the couch. What about the day before? The drive-in, probably. Maybe she would have called in the middle of me sitting on his lap, riding atop him, both of us trying to keep quiet and still enough that the car didn't shake and rock so that everyone around us would know what we were doing.

Neither of those sounds like a very good time for my mother to call.

"Have you seen Ethan?" she asks. "I know you two don't really get along well, but I was hoping we could all do something together soon."

Oh, yes, Ethan and I aren't suppose to get along well, are we? Well, um...

As if to emphasize just how badly we get along, Ethan reaches for my pussy under the blankets. His fingers tease and caress against my lower lips, sending me into a sharp, panicked frenzy. I gasp and shift back on the bed, moving away from him. Oh my God. My mother looks at me like I'm crazy, which I don't blame her for.

To try and hide this, I cough loudly.

"Sorry!" I say. "I think I have allergies or something."

"I'll get something for you at the store," she says, nodding. This is an acceptable answer, apparently.

"I'm not sure where Ethan is, either," I add. "I saw him last night, but I haven't really seen him this morning."

"That's what you get for sleeping in late," my mother says, smiling and pretending to be upset, shaking her head side to side. "I'm sure he's fine. He can take care of himself."

What would I usually say to that? Something rude, maybe. Not too rude, but... Oh, I know.

"He's probably just with some girl," I say. "You know him. He's kind of a jerk."

"Ashley," my mother says, frowning. With a sigh, she adds, "I know you two don't get along too much, but please, don't say things like that. He's just... he's had a hard time, you know? We can both help make that better."

"Hard time?" I ask, laughing. Laughing because I'm not sure how a rich kid could have a hard time of anything, but also because he's definitely been hard this entire time with me. I really want to be nice to him, but honestly he's just a...

A what? A jerk. That's what I've always thought of him as. Arrogant and rude and cocky. That's the Ethan I know.

Or is it? I'm not sure anymore. He's still arrogant and cocky, and a little rude, but I kind of like him the way he's been the past few days.

The past few days, except now that's over. It's done. We have to go back to how we were. We have to be the people everyone expects us to be, and I know exactly what that means for me. I think he must know what it means for him, too.

"It's none of my business," she says to me. "I don't want to start anything. If you want to find out, you should talk to him. Get to know him a little. For better or worse, you're kind of stuck with him now, aren't you? Me and his father aren't going anywhere anytime soon, so you're both going to have to learn to deal with each other. I think you should try reaching out to him, Ashley."

I do. Right then and there. It's not the way my mother means, except maybe it is in some ways, too. I shift my hand under the blankets until I find him, his hand. I take his fingers in mine and he squeezes my hand gently in return.

"Maybe," I say.

"Do you want some breakfast? We left early this morning and haven't had a chance to eat yet. I know it's late. More like brunch, huh?"

"Breakfast or brunch sounds great," I say.

"Pancakes?" my mom asks. "If I see Ethan I'll ask him to make you some? I know how much you like his pancakes. That's something, right? It's a start. See, you two can get along when you want to."

I know what she's saying. I understand what she's trying to do here. I don't think it's helping, though. I think back to when he made me pancakes that day. It wasn't even that long ago. It was practically yesterday. We'd slept together by accident, and I woke up hating him, but then he made pancakes and then he wasn't exactly a jerk, and then he...

And now it's over. Done. We'll never do any of that again.

"That would be nice," I tell my mom.

"Alright. Come down when you can. I'll get everything set up."

I nod and she nods, then she steps out of my room and closes the door behind her.

As soon as she's gone, I sweep back the blankets and hop out of bed. Scampering to the door, I press the button to lock it. I'd rather not have to explain any of this to her or my stepdad, and this is the easiest way I can think of. Lock the door.

Except Ethan's still in here with me. This isn't good, is it?

He's laying in my bed, leaning back, hands behind his head resting on my pillow. And he's naked, too. His foot is covered by blankets, but that's about it. His morning erection stands high and proud. I can't even believe him! Now of all times? My God.

I'm naked, too, though. Maybe he's hard because of that? Can it happen so quickly, just from staring at me naked when I ran to lock my bedroom door? Apparently so!

"What's up?" he says, brow furrowed like he's confused.

"You, apparently!" I say, hushed. I glare pointedly at his erection.

"Cute," he says, smirking. "How about that reaching out thing your mom mentioned? Now seems like a great time to me."

Yes, I realize that sounds innocuous, but Ethan finishes it by waving towards his cock and then making fake jerking off motions. What an... an asshole!

It's kind of sexy and fun in a weird way, too, though.

"You're a jerk," I tell him.

"Yeah, I heard. Nice to know you think so highly of me. You always talk to your mom about me like that?"

"Pretty much," I say. It's kind of true.

"Come back to bed, Princess," Ethan says. "We've got a few more minutes. No need to waste it."

I want to believe him. I truly deeply really really want to believe him, but I can't.

"Ethan, they're back," I say. "We can't do this anymore. We need to stop, and I think we need to start stopping by you going back to your room."

"Yeah," he says. "I get it."

Why does he sound upset? It hurts to hear him talk like that. If anything I should be the one that's upset, right?

"I thought they were going to be gone for a week?" I say.

"Listen," he says. "I thought the same thing. Don't try and pin this on me."

"I'm not pinning anything on you," I say, frowning.

"Yeah, whatever, Princess. Really, I get it. Don't worry." He sounds... angry?

"What's wrong with you?" I ask. I don't mean for it to come out like that, I don't mean for it to sound mean or aggressive, but I know that's exactly how I sound.

I'm at the bed now. I walk closer, closer still, trying to understand. Ethan is standing up, looking at me. Without warning, he grabs me by the waist and tosses me onto the bed, then prowls over me. His knee presses between my legs, keeping them parted for him, and his chest squeezes against mine. He's close. So close that I could kiss him. I want to. I wish things weren't happening the way they are.

I wish we could have woken up on our own, without anyone coming home, and that we could have made love in bed before lazily wandering downstairs and making breakfast in our pajamas. I wish we could have spent the day together. I wish we could have gone swimming. Maybe we could have gone to the beach? It's an hour drive, but that's not too bad. We could have gone to get ice cream, and then picked up food on the way back home.

We could have done the same thing tomorrow. And the day after. We could have done it until we had to stop, except now we need to stop immediately.

My heart hurts. My heart isn't supposed to hurt. Why do I hurt? Ethan's just my... my stepbrother. He's my stepbrother with benefits for the week, except it's over already and it hasn't been a week.

He pulls my thighs apart gently, all while staring at me with that wicked and intense look in his eyes. It's crude and angry and mean, but there's something hiding deep inside. There's something he doesn't want to tell me, but I don't know what it is.

My mother told me to reach out to him. Maybe I should.

I cup his cheeks in my hands and pull him close to kiss him. He softens slightly, and then he sinks into me.

We're doing this. I know it's wrong. It's very wrong right now. He's inside me, though. It feels good. It's perfect and right. He fills me completely in more ways than one. My heart doesn't hurt as much anymore. It feels fixed, less broken. I kiss him and he stays inside me, pressing close.

"I just wanted to feel you one last time," he says. "I'll leave you to your own life now, Princess. You take care, alright?"

What does he mean? What is he saying? I try to kiss him again, but he slowly pulls my hands away and pins them above my head. While I writhe and squirm and struggle to fight against him, he slides his length out of me. He's all the way out now, but I can see him. His cock glistens with my arousal. He's not done yet. He didn't cum. We didn't have sex.

We can't have sex. He's my stepbrother. Our parents are right downstairs. My mom was just in my room. If she had seen him...

"Please," I say, begging him. "Don't go. Ethan, please don't."

"This is how it is," he says, but he doesn't sound like he believes himself. "This is what I do, Princess. You've seen it. You've seen it more than anyone. Don't you remember? All those times I've fucked girls and then ditched them? It's nothing new. I thought you understood what was going to happen. It's the same thing."

"It's not!" I say. He lets go of my hands, but I don't know what to do now. I don't know if I want to grab him and kiss him, or if I want to slap him and hurt him.

He finds his pajama pants and t-shirt on the floor near his side of my bed and puts them on, cocky and slow. It's maddening to watch him do this. It's infuriating! He walks to my bedroom door and twists the doorknob to unlock it.

"See you around," he says. "Maybe we can hang out sometime."

Maybe we can hang out sometime? What the heck does that mean? Why is he doing this? He was just inside of me! I can still see his erection through his loose pajama pants, and all he has to do is step back in my room, close and lock the door behind him, and he can have me again, but he doesn't.

He steps out, he leaves me.

I clench my hands into fists and pound on my bed. It's not! It's not the same! He's not the same! He's...

Maybe he is. This is what all of the other girls thought, too, isn't it? I realize it suddenly, and it hurts even more. He didn't use me. He didn't do anything to me. I knew exactly what sort of person Ethan Colton was going into this, and now he's showing me exactly what sort of person he is again.

I grab one of my pillows and pull it over my mouth, holding it there so it can muffle and drown out my pleading sobs.

"It's not! It's not the same! I don't want it to be the same! I want you to come back, Ethan! I want you to..."

I cry. It's so strange. I was angry when Jake dumped me, but I didn't cry. Ethan and I weren't even really dating, and so why am I crying right now? I don't know. I don't know if I'll ever know.

The only thing I know right now is that I have to get up. I have to get dressed and go downstairs because my mom is back home and she's waiting for me.

I'm smart. I'm an intelligent girl. Lots of people think I'm perfect, at least as far as grades go. They tell me. They say they wish they could do as well as me. I got an almost perfect score on my SATs, graduated high school with perfect grades, said a speech in front of my class about our futures, and received special assignments and initiatives as a freshman in college which is difficult to say the least.

This is the hardest thing I've ever done, though. Nothing before now could have ever prepared me for this. I have to walk downstairs, see my mother, and pretend like nothing from the past few days ever happened.

I have to pretend I didn't accidentally fall in love with Ethan Colton, my stepbrother.

I don't know how this could have happened.

8 - Ethan

Y EAH, FUCK YOU. Fuck off. Just shut the fuck up. I don't want to deal with your shit.

I'm a jerk. I'm a huge fucking asshole. An arrogant fuck. A douchebag. I hurt girls. I know it. I don't want to hurt them. I seriously don't. I just want to show them a good time. I want to be the safe rebound guy. There, are you fucking happy?

That's what I do. That's what I've always done. That's why I don't have relationships. I'm not relationship material. There's plenty of assholes who will take advantage of a girl, especially one who broke up with a guy recently and is on the mend. I think that's really fucking shitty, though.

What I do isn't exactly nice, but I like to think it's nicer than the alternatives. I treat every girl like a fucking Queen, at least for a little while.

Except her. Ashley's my fucking Princess.

Ha! Not anymore! What the fuck happened? Why did they have to come home early? A phone call would have been nice. Hey, son, we're coming home earlier than planned. Hope you're not fucking your stepsister while we're gone! That'd be really fucking weird. Just so you know!

Fuck off. It's not weird. It was fucking perfect until it all went to hell.

What did I expect? I don't fucking know. Not this. Not what happened. And then that look she gave me. It's like she hates me all over again. I didn't think she liked me before now, but I didn't think she hated me, either.

Maybe it's not hate. Hate's a strong word. It's just that we both know we can't do this. I thought maybe we could figure it out. I don't know how. Why the fuck are you asking me?

I thought she locked the door so we could just lounge in bed a little longer. Didn't even have to have sex. I was joking. Yeah, a morning handjob wouldn't be the worst way to wake up, especially with Ashley giving it, but I would have been happy just laying there and cuddling and kissing.

Who am I and what am I doing? This shit is seriously fucked up. Cuddle and kiss? Holy fuck.

We can't. We're done. This girl lives in the same house as me. Her bedroom is just down the hall. It barely takes twenty seconds to go from her room to mine, and yet it's an impossible distance now. She might as well be on the sun with me on fucking... ice planet Pluto or whatever. Is it even a planet? I don't fucking know. It's a bunch of crazy science shit and I never really paid attention to any of it.

You know who would know? Ashley.

You know who I can't fucking talk to right now? Ashley.

You know what I'm fucking doing? Nothing with Ashley.

Almost.

As soon as I leave her room, I go to mine. I try to stay calm. I kind of wish someone saw me. No one does, though. If they did, this might be better. My dad could yell at me. Her mom, too. What the fuck are you doing in my daughter's room? You really want to know, *Mom?* I was fucking her. And I want to fuck her again. How the fuck do you like that?

Nah, I wouldn't do that to her. Ashley doesn't deserve that. Neither does her mom. They're both good people. Better than me. Maybe that's why my dad married her mom. He realized how fucked up we were, and how good they were, and he thought we could become better people with them in our lives.

My dad did. He's good now. Better. He tries. I can't put up with it. It's been too long.

I lock my door to keep her from coming in. I don't know if she'll try, but it wouldn't be the craziest thing a girl's done after I ditched them. Ashley knew what was coming. Yeah, it came sooner than I would have liked, but she knew.

I knew, too. Why can't I stop thinking about her, then?

I'm hard. I'm not proud of that, but I am, and I have to go downstairs, too. I have to deal with it, so I deal with it. I stomp into my private bathroom and turn on the hot water to take a shower. I strip and get in and under the water. There's good memories in here. And bad ones.

I think of that first day. I guess it's the day after, if we're being technical. She came in here naked, ready as fuck. It took everything I could not to fuck her right then and there. Take it fucking slow, Ethan. Go slow with her.

I'm not slow right now. I wrap my fingers around my cock and stroke fast, thinking about her. I can feel her arousal on me still, coating my shaft. It's sexy as fuck, and it's the last time this will ever happen.

I cum. It doesn't take long. I picture her in the shower with me that first day. She looked a little scared, but interested. I wanted to be careful with her. Those were my thoughts when I saw her then. Be careful with her, you prick. Don't fucking hurt her.

Look how well that turned out? I'm a real fucking saint over here.

You'd think that masturbating would have gotten me over this shit, at least for now, but it doesn't. I clean off in the shower and start to wash myself, but a few minutes later I'm hard as fuck again. Holy fucking shit, are you for real?

Yeah, I guess so.

I try to ignore it, but I can't. I start thinking about eating her out. Her first time. Fuck, she's delicious. I love the taste of her pussy. I did *not* get enough of that. I missed a real fucking good opportunity right there.

Again. Fingers. Cock. Hand. Stroke.

It takes a little longer, but I coat the fuck out of the shower wall with my cum. It washes off with a quick spray of water, and then there's nothing left but me and my hate and anger and rage. Fuck this shit.

Conditioner. Just put the goddamn conditioner in your hair, get a fucking towel, and get dressed, Ethan. I have to yell at myself just to get anything done.

Mostly works. Almost doesn't.

Yeah, again. You know the drill. How fucking long have I been in this shower?

The third time seems to stick. I can't get it up anymore after that. How long's that going to last? I feel like as soon as I see her I'm just going to turn into a walking erection again, so who the fuck knows?

The last time I didn't even think about sex. I thought about us last night, when we were cuddling on the couch and eating pizza. She was laughing at something on TV and then she turned to me and I saw a sparkle in her eyes.

What did she say to me when I got out of the hot tub to go get the pizza? I remember it. I'm never going to forget it.

Kiss?

I kissed her then. I kissed her when she was laughing, too. She had a little dab of pizza sauce on the corner of her lips, and I licked it off, then kissed her. Quick. That's it. She blushed and then rubbed her cheek against mine. It was cute. A little different. I don't know why she did that, but I liked it.

Yeah, real good spank bank material, huh? Masturbate to kissing a girl? Not even a fucking passionate kiss, just something soft and sweet and playful.

I don't fucking know. It sure as hell worked, anyways. What do you want me to say?

I get out of the shower and dry off fast. I'm soft now. Fucking finally. I grab a pair of underwear. Nah, two. I need to restrain myself and this should hopefully do the trick. I put on both pairs, then a pair of jeans, too. Takes some work to get that shit on. I don't recommend wearing two pairs of underwear, alright? I'm just looking out for later when I inevitably see Ashley and get an instant hard-on.

Life is difficult and I hate it.

I toss on a t-shirt, too, then some socks and shoes, and head downstairs. The least I can do is say hi to my dad and her mom and have some breakfast.

That's it, though. I can't stay here. Not with her.

I just can't.

Mia Clark

9 - Ashley

EVERYTHING IS STIFLED. Usually when we all eat together, it's like this, but it feels worse now. I want to sit next to Ethan. I want to reach out and touch his hand randomly. I want to kiss him. That's what we did last night when we were eating pizza. We weren't at the table, but we were in the living room watching TV, and I could do whatever I wanted. If I wanted to kiss him, I could kiss him. If I wanted to touch him, I could touch him. It didn't matter how or where. There were no obstacles between us.

We're sitting at the kitchenette table off of the kitchen, me and him and my mom and his dad. It's bigger than a regular kitchenette table, and we're all spaced apart more evenly. I'm sitting with my mom and his dad to either side of me, and Ethan is opposite me.

I could touch him, I guess. With my foot. I could stretch my leg under the table and touch my foot to his and no one would know, but it doesn't seem right. I don't think he'll like it. He won't even look at me.

"How's school going?" his dad asks him. "Keeping up your grades for football, right?"

"Yeah," Ethan says, practically grunting the word. "Fine."

"That's great," my mom says, smiling. "Ashley, I'm sure you're doing fine, too?"

"As always," Ethan's dad says, grinning. "Maybe you could help Ethan study during summer break?"

"Sure!" I say. I probably sound too eager, but I don't care. "If... if he wants? I don't mind."

"Yeah, no," Ethan says. "It's summer break for a reason. I need a rest."

Everything's quiet after that. No one else knows what to say. I eat in silence, and so does Ethan. He still won't look at me. His gaze is straight in his plate, glaring at his food. Pancakes and scrambled eggs and sausage. The pancakes are good, but they aren't as good as his.

"I was thinking about making fruit smoothies later," I say out of the blue. I try to say it confidently and self-assured, but I stumble halfway through when Ethan jerks his head up, finally looking at me. He's... angry? I'm not sure.

"If... if anyone wants one..." I add, uncertain.

"That would be great, Ashley," Ethan's dad says. "It's been nice out lately, and that'd be a refreshing treat after the week your mother and I had. It was a good trip, but a lot of business to deal with."

"Yeah, you said you'd be gone for a week, but now you're back," Ethan says. "What's up with that?"

"What, did I ruin your plans for a house party?" his dad says. "I thought we went over this when you trashed the house in high school. Just because you're in college now doesn't change anything."

"No, he--" I start to say.

Ethan interrupts me. "Yeah, so what if I was?"

"I thought you were changing," his father says. "You've been a lot less rebellious lately. The past couple of years were great, Ethan. Everything I've heard from you about your first year at college sounds good, too. Apparently you're determined to make me hate you, though. I don't, and I don't know why you want me to so badly."

"I think that's enough of that," my mom says. "Everyone's just on edge. It must have been hard for the two of them coming home and having to fend for themselves for a couple of days."

The two of them. That's us. Ethan and I were alone. I didn't feel alone. Did he?

"You could really try spending more time with Ashley, Ethan," his dad says. "I think you both have more in common than you might think."

"Oh yeah?" Ethan says. "So, what, we can start having family game nights or something? Play Hungry Fucking Hippos at the table, laughing, and dipping broccoli florets into creamy Ranch sauce? You want me to wear a fucking sweater vest while I'm at it? I'll go pick one up today. I'll get right on it."

His father starts to say something, but my mother reaches across the table to calm my stepdad down. Everything is quiet again, but there's miles between all of us. It's staring me right in the face, too.

I can't be Ethan's friend. I can never be his friend. I don't know if he was lying before, about that and about everything, but I know it's not possible. Our parents will always come between us, figuratively and literally. My mom's hand reaching for Ethan's father isn't just some literary allusion that English majors will study about while reading the book of our lives, it's an actual physical thing that's happening to me right now.

I look across the table at Ethan, look over my mother's arm that's stretched between us. He's looking at me now, too. Finally he's looking at me. I have so much I want to tell him, but I can't, so I hope he sees it in my eyes. I hope for it so much. I want him to understand.

I want him to know I love him. Even if it's just for a little bit, I love him and I loved him.

He turns away, fast. His plate is still half filled with food, but he picks it up and brings it to the trash, then dumps the rest of his meal in the garbage before tossing his plate in the sink.

"I'm going out," he says to no one in particular. "Sorry for causing trouble."

My mom gives Ethan's dad a look. "I didn't mean to put so much stress on you immediately after we got back," his dad says. "I just want the best for you. You know that, right?"

"Yeah, sure thing, Dad. I get it."

It's the same way he spoke to me this morning. It's almost the same thing he said, too.

"Let's have dinner together tonight," my mom says. "We can stay in or go out. What do you say?"

"That sounds nice," I say. With more confidence than I feel, I add, "I would like to try and get to know you better, Ethan. We can be friends if--"

He stops me. It's just a quick look, but it hurts more than anything. It hurts because he looks so hurt right now, too. It hurts because he doesn't want anyone to know that he hurts.

"Maybe," he says. "I'll try to be around for dinner. That's it." To me, he says, "You aren't so bad, but I don't think we can be friends. Not like you want." After a second's pause, he adds, "*Princess*."

I bite my bottom lip to stop myself from crying. Ethan turns around and leaves after that. A few seconds later I hear the roar of one of the cars in the garage coming to life. I don't know a lot about cars, but I remember how they sound, and he's taking the one we took to the drive-in movie theatre the other night. Does that mean anything, or am I reading into it too much? Is he trying to tell me something?

I finish eating while my mom and stepdad talk about some things. They keep looking over at me every so often, but I don't want to talk to them. I don't have anything to say, really. I wish these were Ethan's pancakes. I wish we'd made them together this morning.

"Honey, is everything alright?" my mom asks. "You look upset."

"If it's about Ethan, he's just--" my stepfather starts to say.

I stop him. I can't. I can't talk about Ethan.

"Jake broke up with me," I say. I start to cry, too. I let out all of the pain and anguish I've been feeling this entire time, setting loose my tears. "Right before I came back here for summer break, Jake broke up with me."

My mom takes in a deep breath, a sort of backwards gasp of shock. She covers her mouth with one hand. Ethan's father looks around awkwardly, unsure what to do. He gets up and takes our empty plates, bringing them to the sink.

"I'll let you handle this," he says to my mom. "If you need me, I'm here, though. You know that, right, Ashley?"

I nod. They think I'm crying because of Jake.

I'm not. I'm crying because of Ethan.

It's a good distraction, though. It's better for them to think I'm crying because of something else.

This is the best way for me to handle this situation right now. It's the only way I can.

"What happened?" my mom asked. "I thought you two were doing well?"

"I mean, we were doing alright,"I say. "We went on dates a couple times a week. We... we had sex, Mom. I..."

She smiles. "It's alright. You can tell me anything."

Can I? I doubt it.

"He told me that he didn't want to wait the entire summer to have sex again, so he was breaking up with me, but we could get back together later."

"Oh," my mom says. She wrinkles her brow, unsure how to process this. To be honest, I didn't know how to process it when I heard it, either.

"Yup. Nice of him, huh?"

"Long distance relationships are hard," my mother says. "I'm sure that's what he meant. He didn't mean that he wanted to have sex with other girls, Ashley. He just wanted to have a nice summer, and he wanted you to have a nice summer, too. If you were both sad about missing each other, it'd be hard, right? That's why he said you could start dating again when you got back to college. I'm sure of it."

I'm glad my mom is sure of it, because I'm not. I know that's not what he meant. It's nice that she's trying to protect me, though. It's nice that she cares.

"I know it's hard," she says. "Maybe it's weird to hang out with your mom, but we can if you want. Do you need some new summer clothes? We could go shopping."

I laugh a little, caught between that and crying. That's what Julia and I did, too. I even bought some sexy lingerie. I didn't have a chance to show Ethan. I wanted to, but now I can't.

"Let me go get ready and we'll go," she says. "If you're up for it? If you want, we can stay in, too. Maybe go swimming instead? Just relax by the pool all day? Your stepfather could be our cabana boy and bring us drinks?" She smiles and wipes the tears from my cheeks.

It's funny. Kind of funny. I can't even imagine Ethan's dad doing that, but I bet he would, even though he's rich. He's nice. I don't know why Ethan doesn't get along with him, but maybe that's it. Maybe he's just nice to me? I've never thought about it that way before. I don't know if it's true. I don't think it is.

"I'd rather not go swimming," I say. If we do, I don't think I'd be able to think of anything but Ethan. I'm sure that the drinks my mother mentioned would be of the non-alcoholic variety, but I don't think I'd be able to stop thinking of that fateful night with Ethan, either. "Shopping would be nice, though."

I sniffle and wipe away the rest of my tears. My mom smiles and claps her hands together.

"It's decided then," she says. "Twenty minutes! I'll be quick. Then we'll go."

"Where are we going?" Ethan's father asks, returning from his quick escape.

"You aren't going anywhere," my mother says, grinning and pointing her finger at him. "Me and Ashley are going shopping, though. We're going to spend the day together. It's a girl thing. Sorry, dear, but you aren't invited."

I grin at their playful banter. It's fun. "You can come if you want to," I say. "Maybe try on some summer dresses?"

"Ah, I'll have to pass," he says, chuckling. "I'm afraid that no matter what I try on, my butt is definitely going to look big. It'll never work. You two ladies have fun, though."

I giggle. This is normal. This is how we're supposed to be. This is what I'm supposed to do.

I'm not supposed to have sex with my stepbrother. I'm not supposed to have a stepbrother with benefits.

I was never supposed to fall in love with Ethan Colton. I never intended to. It just sort of happened.

It's done now, though. I need to move on with my life.

Right?

A NOTE FROM MIA

OH NO...

Their parents came home early, which is definitely going to put a crimp in Ethan and Ashley's plans, but maybe it's for the best? They've been worrying over this happening eventually, and then it happened, so... they knew it would, right?

I don't think it's that easy, though. It's kind of sad, because there's not really any closure there. I'd say that's kind of important for any relationship, but especially one like this.

Hm... but it's not over, so they've still got time. Two more books worth of time, in fact. Definitely an opportunity for some more fun and excitement, and there is a lot of that happening in a short amount of time, too.

The next book is probably my favorite out of all of these. I don't want to spoil it for you, but a lot happens, and it's really fun. Yes, their parents are home now, but they might still have some rules to follow. Maybe they can make up a few more rules, too. We'll have to see!

These were some really fun books to write, though. Ashley and Ethan are interesting characters, and I enjoyed being able to play around and get into their heads. The back and forth between them two is my favorite part, and I hope you enjoy it a lot, as well.

There's more coming shortly, too, though. I hope you enjoy the rest of the series as much as you've enjoyed the books up until now.

If you do like these books, I'd love if you rated and reviewed them. Do you think Ethan can change his bad boy ways? He kind of reverted a little at the end there, but I think there's still some home for him. What about Ashley, though? It was easy to kind of forget about being a good girl when only Ethan was around, but can she keep being something of a bad girl now that it's not just her and Ethan at home again? Two very difficult questions right there.

I hope you're liking this series so far. There's more to come, don't worry!

Thanks for reading, and I'll see you soon! (next book!)

~Mia

ABOUT THE AUTHOR

Mia likes to have fun in all aspects of her life. Whether she's out enjoying the beautiful weather or spending time at home reading a book, a smile is never far from her face. She's prone to randomly laughing at nothing in particular except for whatever idea amuses her at any given moment.

Sometimes you just need to enjoy life, right?

She loves to read, dance, and explore outdoors. Chamomile tea and bubble baths are two of her favorite things. Flowers are especially nice, and she could get lost in a garden if it's big enough and no one's around to remind her that there are other things to do.

She lives in New Hampshire, where the weather is beautiful and the autumn colors are amazing.

Manufactured by Amazon.ca
Bolton, ON

12874355R00055